FRANKIE FOX

GIRL SPY

READY, SET, SPY

A Lothian Children's Book

Published in Australia and New Zealand in 2015
by Hachette Australia
Level 17, 207 Kent Street, Sydney NSW 2000
www.hachettechildrens.com.au

10 9 8 7 6 5 4 3 2 1

National Library of Australia
Cataloguing-in-Publication data

Poshoglian, Yvette, author.
Ready, set, spy/Yvette Poshoglian.

978 0 7344 1568 4 (paperback)

For primary school age.

Girls – Juvenile fiction.
Spy stories.
Children's stories.

A823.4

Cover and internal illustrations by Jacqui Davis
Cover design by Mathematics
Text design by Bookhouse, Sydney
Typeset in 11/17 Stempel Garamond
Printed and bound in Australia by Griffin Press, Adelaide, an Accredited
ISO AS/NZS 14001:2009 Environmental Management System printer

READY, SET, SPY

YVETTE POSHOGLIAN

LOTHIAN
Children's Books

CHAPTER ONE

GRIFFIN HOUSE, GRIFFIN CLOSE, HARBOUR CITY
▼

Frankie Fox put *The Spy's Handbook* down. Her brain hurt. No matter how many times she read the secret note scribbled inside the front cover, it still didn't make sense. Frankie couldn't help but think that the strange message held the key to ... something. She looked one more time.

TCITNAL HREHGNE EESESE! STOWOA ELNIFG

What on earth did it mean? It wasn't another language. It didn't make any more sense when she read it out loud. Frankie even tried to read it backwards. She wrote the letters down on a piece of paper, cut them up, and rearranged them on her desk. They made even less sense than before. The exclamation mark, however, made it seem like some kind of warning. Next to her, Boss, the laziest West Highland White Terrier in the world, snuffled in his sleep.

Frankie gave him a pat and watched him drool happily in a basket built specially for lazy fur balls. Every spy needed a sidekick, or at the very least, a guard dog. Boss was great at eating and snoring, but he was most definitely NOT spy material. He was tiny. The most energetic Frankie ever saw him was when he wasn't given seconds at dinnertime. Now as she watched him, little tufts of white hair rippled in the breeze as he snored.

Frankie had always wanted to be a spy. Other girls wanted dolls and ponies for their birthdays, but Frankie had always asked for things like binoculars or a waterproof watch.

She'd have to ask her father about the book. It had mysteriously arrived on her desk in the boathouse a week ago in a plain brown paper bag, held together by a thick rubber band. A sticky note had been attached to the front of the bag:

For the attention of Francesca Fox:
I found this in my library. It belongs in your library
now.
Dad
P.S. IELYOOVU

Her father had never been very good at wrapping gifts. Or writing personal notes.

He always signed off with the first code Frankie had ever learned to crack, when she was in kindergarten. A simple coded message, it was a way of writing a message within a message. At first glance, it appeared just a jumble of words.

IELYOOVU

But when she broke it down, every second letter made up the message. The first, third, fifth and seventh letters spelled I LOV . . . Frankie went back to the second, fourth, sixth and eighth letters.

EYOU

Put together, it spelled ILOVEYOU, or I LOVE YOU.

Frankie Fox – aged 11, resident of Harbour City, student at Chumsworth School for Girls – was teaching herself to become a spy, one step at a time. The book hadn't even made it to her own library yet – a handcrafted wooden bookcase that had been built into one side of the boathouse where she lived. It hadn't moved from her bed, where she read it propped up on her lap late every night, or her desk, where she pored over it every morning before school. Within a week, Frankie had read the old red, tattered volume cover to cover.

The handbook had over five hundred yellowing pages, and was printed in dark ink that seeped at the edge of some of the pages. There was no author name, just a table of contents. Some of the page numbers had been circled randomly throughout the book. A sheet of tactical moves sent to her by her chess coach, the Armenian Grandmaster Robert Hagopian, was her dog-eared bookmark.

The Spy's Handbook could not have come to Frankie at a better time. For the last eighteen and a half days, Frankie had believed she was being watched. Or followed. Or both.

On the advice of the handbook, Frankie had set up a basic tripwire at the entrance to the boathouse. This involved placing a network of wire coathangers on the back of the boathouse doors to announce intruders, and applying a fine dusting of talcum powder on the floor to show up footprints. She couldn't be sure if she was being followed, but sometimes things were just out of *whack*. A nosy old man with a walking stick had been strolling along Griffin Close. But it wasn't a street you passed through on your way to somewhere else – people only came to Griffin Close if they had a reason to be there. And the old man didn't look like he really needed the walking stick at all. Also, there had been a young man dressed as a workman pretending to mend the neighbours' fence but he hadn't fixed anything at all. Frankie knew that someone had been in her room, too. She was determined to catch them and find out why they had been snooping. Frankie had always wanted to be a spy; now the handbook would make her an expert.

Frankie and Boss lived in a big house called Griffin on a quiet, suburban street called Griffin Close. Frankie's room was separate to the actual house of Griffin. It was 178 stairs away from the main house, down a large cliff and perched on the harbour of Harbour City itself. She lived with her father and Hanna, their housekeeper. Her mother had died when she was just a baby. Neither her

father or Hanna came to the boathouse very often, as they were under Frankie's strict instructions to STAY AWAY.

But Frankie was sure that someone had been in her room recently because her trophies had been moved. She always lined them up to face her in bed. Frankie loved trophies the way some girls love teddy bears. Her Under-8 Fencing trophy was facing the wrong way. Her Under-7 Motocross Challenge trophy was upside down – the small bronze figure on the bike now looked like it had been involved a major crash. Her bathroom mirror had also been tampered with. It now hung at a strange angle – close enough to how it had been originally, but there was still enough of a difference to set Frankie on edge.

A real electric tripwire ran the perimeter of Griffin House. Once, Frankie had zinged herself on it as a little girl. Security cameras kept a roving eye on Griffin Close. Sometimes, Frankie felt like her father wanted to cut them off from the rest of the world. Fergus Fox was very famous, and very rich. He was a brilliant scientist who ran a secretive set of labs on Fortress Island and suspected that lots of people wanted to steal his secrets, or his money. Or both.

This was Frankie's first Saturday off from fencing this term. Her best friend Rani was playing netball this season, but Frankie had chosen fencing because she thought it was a more useful skill for a future spy.

Frankie and her father had planned a day scrambling around the island. He had to drop some paperwork into his office and then the rest of the day was theirs for kayaking and exploring the maze of old gun batteries, tunnels and cranes. The whole place was spooky. Frankie loved it. She knew her dad did, too.

Frankie looked around for her waterproof shoes. The place was a mess. A pair of binoculars hung on a strap over her cupboard door. A telescope sat by the window, its lens trained on Fortress Island. A microscope and slides holding a squashed beetle and a collection of leaves sat on her bookshelf. Apart from *The Spy's Handbook,* Frankie was reading two other books: *A Short History of DNA* (it was actually over seven hundred pages long – not short at all) and *Cryptology for Dummies.* Her shoes were buried under yesterday's dirty clothes. She found a pair of scrunched-up board shorts and her favourite T-shirt and was ready in record time.

The wire coathangers jangled at the door. 'Morning,' her father said, pushing the boathouse door open. He was dressed in a sharp blue business suit.

'You can't go kayaking in that horrible suit,' Frankie said.

'I'm sorry, Frankie —' he began.

'You can't hang out today,' Frankie finished for him.

Fergus Fox looked embarrassed.

'You're *always* working,' Frankie moaned.

'I'm sorry, Francesca,' Fergus said, giving her a big bear hug. 'I wish it didn't have to be this way.'

Frankie pulled away. 'Can't I come too?' she asked.

'It's not safe —' Fergus Fox began, but stopped himself. 'I mean, I can't spare any time today.'

It's not safe. The words sounded disturbing. Her father had not even meant to say them out loud. Frankie's spy sense went on full alert. 'Doesn't matter,' she said gruffly. 'I'm pretty busy anyway.' Frankie had planned to ask her father about the handbook, but now she was in a bad mood. But mostly, she wished she knew what her father was really doing in those long, lonely hours without her.

Fergus looked at his daughter's blonde curls pulled back into a ponytail. *She is exactly like her mother,* he thought. *Strong and proud. And very, very clever.*

'Alright,' he said finally. 'I'll see you tomorrow at breakfast. Hanna's upstairs. Why don't you keep her company?' His footsteps clattered out down the boat ramp towards the small motor cruiser that bobbed in the water outside the boathouse. The engine of the *Lucky Jo* throbbed into life and she watched him take off through the bay towards Harbour City and Fortress Island, leaving his daughter and a wake of white water behind.

CHAPTER TWO

Surveillance is an important aspect of spying. It can be as simple as keeping an eye on your neighbours, watching for new cars in your neighbourhood, or making a note of strange coincidences. Remember: nothing is a coincidence. There may be something more sinister at work.

THE SPY'S HANDBOOK

GRIFFIN HOUSE, GRIFFIN CLOSE, HARBOUR CITY
▼

Last week, Frankie had noticed large removalists' vans with the words '*COAST-TO-COAST MOVERS – We turn your world (not your goods) upside down*' choking up their small street. A man, a woman and a boy around her own age inspected the process, while Frankie had watched, hidden in the dense front garden of Griffin.

The new neighbours shared a fence with the Foxes, their house concealed by a mess of tangled weeds, ferns and another decrepit boathouse on their side. Tall ghost gums separated the occupants of number 2 (her house) and number 4 Griffin Close (the neighbours' house).

Frankie thought about spying on the new neighbours again, to practise her skills and distract herself from her disappointment about her father. But she decided that cracking the code in *The Spy's Handbook* was more important. If the message revealed something top secret, it had to be kept safe.

Just before lunchtime, the wire hangers jostled at her door again. A familiar face lined with wrinkles peered in.

'Hi, Hanna,' Frankie said. Hanna was their house-keeper, but to Frankie she felt more like a favourite grandmother and aunty rolled into one.

'I made your favourite,' Hanna said, lowering a plate of steaming hot lasagne onto Frankie's desk. Hanna used the funicular, a small railway built into the cliff. It was operated by levers and was good for hauling things up and down the cliff face instead of carrying them. Hanna's joints were no good for climbing stairs anymore, and she hardly ever came down to the boathouse these days. Today must have been a good day for her.

Boss hovered, his nose detecting the cheesy goo. His little face waited in anticipation of his favourite food.

'And here's a special plate for the Boss,' she said, patting the dog on the head. Boss attacked the lasagne. It was gone in seconds.

'I'm glad I don't get down here very often,' Hanna said, inspecting Frankie's mess. Frankie's room was private and out of bounds. Hanna would have the place tidied in no time at all.

'What's this?' asked Hanna, looking at the copy of *The Spy's Handbook*.

'Dad gave it to me,' she said.

'It's very interesting,' she said, glancing at the code inside but saying nothing. After flicking through it, Hanna put it down and watched as Frankie grabbed it back.

Hanna kissed Frankie on the cheek. 'Enjoy your lunch,' she said, before retreating to the funicular and throwing its levers into gear.

•

Two stops above the boathouse, Hanna hobbled inside and double-checked the front door. She straightened her legs. Fergus Fox wasn't due home for hours and Frankie was nestled in her room.

Hanna punched in the code to her private quarters on the first floor and switched on her TV, locking her own door carefully behind her. The TV didn't show *Who Wants to Be a Squillionaire?* Instead, it showed inside Frankie's boathouse from a secret camera hidden behind the bathroom mirror. Microphones had been placed in her trophies. Hanna's eyes narrowed as she watched Frankie return to the book.

'That spy handbook,' she growled, moving through her room and taking a seat on a stool in front of her dressing table. 'Frankie's getting smarter by the day.' She took off her granny jewellery and nudged a small vase holding a bunch of long-dead dried flowers. The dresser's mirror pane slid open. Her mind raced – how could she stop Frankie from finding out too much?

The false back revealed a small tablet computer and a large array of tools. There was a selection of pens with built-in cameras, a body armour vest and a lipstick tube that doubled as a pistol. In Hanna's ten years of working for the Foxes, she had not yet had to use them.

'Soon,' she whispered. 'The time is near.' The tablet flashed into life and a face appeared. 'Reporting for duty,' said Hanna to the face on the screen.

CHAPTER THREE

Gathering intelligence takes time. Breaks in the pattern of normal life reveal themselves when you least expect it. Keep your eyes open and your wits about you. If you think someone is following you, then you are probably being followed.

THE SPY'S HANDBOOK

SCIENCE LAB 2, CHUMSWORTH SCHOOL FOR GIRLS, HARBOUR CITY

▼

It was a warm Tuesday afternoon. Frankie gingerly lifted the wires attached to the small black battery pack with her needle-nose pliers. She touched her silver eagles' wings for good luck and tucked the necklace under her school shirt collar. The necklace was her good luck charm, but she couldn't quite remember where it had come from.

Frankie was running out of time. Her eyes flicked to the countdown. Ten seconds. Was it the red or the green wire that she was supposed to cut? Anxious eyes watched her around the room. Sweat broke on her upper lip. The back of her neck was damp, her blonde curls pulled back. Frankie was a smidge shorter than the other girls in her year at Chumsworth. Her green eyes narrowed as she focused on the task at hand. Breathing deeply, Frankie selected the green wire. She snipped lightly, exposing the inside tubing of the green cord attached to the battery pack.

Yes!

The red flashing light stopped and the class breathed out. 'Congratulations, Miss Fox. Well done,' Miss Porter looked at her with a mix of pride and astonishment. A girl of Frankie's age wasn't supposed to be able to disarm a fake bomb, especially one with three tripwires planted in it. Miss Porter had made the task extra hard, and it took a logical brain, a firm hand, and nerves of steel to do what Frankie had just done. Miss Porter had chosen Frankie to defuse the bomb, while the other girls did much easier tasks.

Frankie wiped her brow. She allowed herself to feel a small burst of pleasure. Clara Vale, the most popular girl in her class, glared at her. But Miss Porter was still

looking at her in amazement and Frankie felt warm down to the tips of her toes.

Miss Porter had only arrived at Chumsworth that term. She was nothing like any of Frankie's other teachers, who were all boring and sensible. Along with teaching them the periodic table, she made them do experiments that were sometimes very odd. What 11-year-old would ever have to defuse a bomb? Miss Porter also rode a motorbike to school, which Frankie thought was the coolest thing of all. Now, Frankie had passed her latest test with flying colours.

'Guess you got lucky,' sniggered Clara Vale. Clara was the school princess and as slimy as a bag of snakes. Luckily for Clara, the bell rang and Frankie grabbed her backpack and pushed her way out of the stuffy science lab.

'Have you been defusing bombs in your spare time?' A calm voice said behind her. It was Rani, her best friend. 'That was awesome!'

The two girls were joined in the corridor by their other friends.

'How did you do that?' asked Zan, her brown eyes sparkling.

Cat high-fived Frankie. 'You are so cool!' she said.

'Thanks.' Frankie blushed. 'It was nothing, really.' So she was good at solving riddles and disarming bombs. Rani was great at netball and *Military Ops*. Clara was good at using a hair-straightener and playing tennis. Those two things were particularly important at Chumsworth. They were the things that made you popular. Being the daughter of a strange scientist and now having a reputation as a bomb-defuser were definitely NOT.

'Your dad's in the news again,' Rani said, showing her tablet to Frankie. Her father was shaking hands with the prime minister. 'Billionaire genius wins government contract', the headline announced. The article had been posted only an hour ago. Frankie scanned the story. She had been brushing up on her speed reading. It didn't reveal any more about her father or what he was working on. Why was he involved with the government? Once more, she wished she got to spend more time with him. But it was impossible. He had to work and she had to go to school.

'He probably works for the Alliance,' said Clara, overhearing the conversation. Her cronies laughed as Clara pushed past Frankie and her friends in the hall. Frankie huffed, her cheeks flaring red in anger. She really couldn't stand Clara. But more than anything, she hated the Alliance and what they did.

The Alliance was always in the news. It was a mysterious organisation that was growing in strength all over the world. It was a group committed to creating havoc. No one knew where they were based or who their leader was. They had shut down power stations in Eastern Europe, causing blackouts for months at a time. Recently, they had created chaos in the air by jamming air traffic control frequencies in the USA. Some said that Harbour City was their next target, but no one could be sure what the Alliance had planned.

'Don't worry about Clara,' Rani whispered. 'I'll see you in English.'

'Okay – see you later,' Frankie said.

Then Rani was gone and Frankie was left thinking about the horrible Alliance, instead of thinking about more pleasant things, like Rani's sleepover that was coming up on the weekend.

The rest of the day passed slowly. Frankie was glad to finally get on the bus home, but as soon as she stepped on her spy radar went on high alert. The regular bus driver was not there. He had never missed a day of work since she'd started at Chumsworth. The replacement driver was a young woman.

'Bus pass, please,' the new driver said. In her mind she logged away the new information. She saw the woman's pinched nose, sharp blue eyes and a wisp of brown hair under her bus driver's hat.

The driver looked at the photo ID, matching the photo of Frankie's white-blonde, curly hair and green eyes to the figure that stood in front of her. Students buzzed around them, the noise rising to a din of voices talking about shopping, netball and the upcoming holidays.

All the good seats were taken by the time the driver handed back her pass. Frankie reluctantly made her way down to the back seat. Rani had trumpet lessons on Tuesdays and wasn't on the bus home, so Frankie was on her own. She wished she had more friends. There were other nice girls at Chumsworth, but she wasn't as close to them as she was to Rani. They'd been best friends since kindergarten. Rani almost knew Frankie better than she knew herself.

She ignored the large houses and perfect manicured lawns rolling by and thought about *The Spy's Handbook*. As the bus made its way up her street, she stood, peeling her sticky school uniform from the back of her legs.

Frankie was normally the only kid who got off at this stop. But today, a boy wearing a St Paul's uniform stepped off too, shuffling behind her.

'Aren't you going to say hi?' the boy called out to Frankie. He stood at the driveway of the house next door. Frankie looked at his angular face, black hair and pale, grey eyes. 'I saw you watching us the other day.'

Frankie opened her mouth but no words came out. She was embarrassed. If she couldn't snoop on the neighbours properly, what hope did she have of becoming a real spy?

'I'm James Jensen. People call me JJ,' he said, shoving his fringe out of his eyes. 'I used to live here. We moved away and now we're back.'

Frankie nodded. 'Welcome back,' she said. 'I'm Frankie Fox.' She didn't offer him any further inform-ation. Her spy sense told her not to share too much information with the strange new boy. She ran her hand down the tail of the figure etched into the old sandstone wall that surrounded the house. The figure was a griffin, the mythical beast that protected Fergus Fox's treasures – his work and Frankie.

Glancing back in JJ's direction, Frankie buzzed at the gate. The security screen flicked on briefly and Frankie felt the bright red laser scan over her face. The doors began to swing open. JJ seemed very familiar. It was almost as if she knew him from a long time ago . . .

CHAPTER FOUR

Spies change their appearances regularly. Sometimes it requires an outfit change or even a change of hair colour. They also use their surroundings to their advantage. Rainy weather can hide your trail. Smoke, fog and haze can also offer opportunities for escape.

THE SPY'S HANDBOOK

GRIFFIN HOUSE, GRIFFIN CLOSE, HARBOUR CITY
▼

'Who were you talking to?' a cheery voice called. It was Hanna, pottering in the kitchen, fiddling at the countertop. Frankie was convinced Hanna had eyes in the back of her head. Frankie dumped her backpack on the dining table, then headed in to see her.

'Our new neighbour. He just moved here. Or moved back. Or something,' Frankie said, stealing a piece of carrot.

Hanna stopped chopping vegetables and angled her body away from Frankie. Quickly, she made some notes on a pad of paper. Hanna was doing this more and more lately. Nothing escaped Frankie's gaze.

'What are you writing?' Frankie asked. 'Do you need help?'

'My memory's going,' Hanna replied quickly. She looked a bit embarrassed and Frankie felt bad for asking. Poor Hanna didn't like it that she was getting older. Frankie decided to change the subject.

'Wonder if Dad remembers him? I don't. Is Dad eating with us?'

Hanna didn't reply, but placed the pencil down slowly and slid the paper into her pocket. Frankie's heart sank. 'He's on Fortress Island, again, isn't he?' she said.

'Yes, dear,' Hanna said. 'I'm sorry,' she added. She gave Frankie a quick cuddle, then went back to chopping vegetables.

Missing her dad, Frankie walked down the 178 steps from the top of the main house, down the cliff to her bedroom. Checking to see that the powder lay undisturbed, she skipped over the entrance and looked around her room. It appeared untouched. But that didn't mean that someone hadn't been there.

Warily, she went online and finished her chess game with Grandmaster Hagopian. As usual, she lost. His moustachioed face flashed on screen. 'Next time, Frankie,' he said gently. 'Your counter-attack needs work. You are getting very, very close.' He wasn't the kind of teacher to let a child win to make them feel good about themselves. Chess was life to the Grandmaster – he saw the world through a chessboard and he wanted Frankie to as well.

The chess lessons had been a gift for her tenth birthday. For her most recent birthday, her eleventh, Frankie and her dad had gone quad biking in a nature reserve where the people of Harbour City went to hike, camp and picnic. It was an outdoors kind of city.

Her dad had booked out the entire circuit for them. Frankie remembered the sting of diesel oil in her nose, the rush of climbing the tracks, being airborne and speeding over soft hills of dirt. He had taught her how to drift, and Frankie stayed on the whole time without falling off once. Her dad had been so proud of her. But now he just worked all the time. They hadn't done anything together since the quad biking.

Restless, Frankie peered into the high-powered telescope set up at the window. Summer afternoons often left the city shrouded in a blanket of shimmering heat. Fortress Island came into sight, its familiar buildings and cranes bisecting the air.

'C'mon, Boss,' she called quickly. 'If Dad won't come to us – we'll go to him.'

Frankie pulled the kayak down the ramp and into the water. She pushed the boat against the flow of the harbour and Boss jumped in. The heavy orange tub was perfect for night paddling. Daylight faded around them. Boss's ears twitched in the wind, his tongue lolling. Boss had always loved the water, even when he was just a puppy.

Lights from the huge waterfront homes twinkled on and off as she paddled, the light bouncing and streaking off the ripples in the harbour. In the growing dark she could see the glare of TVs, a family sitting on their deck having a barbecue; things that made her feel both happy and sad. She couldn't remember the last time she and Dad and Hanna had sat out on the deck of Griffin House together.

For as long as she could remember, Frankie had been peering into other people's homes. What did they eat for dinner? Who set the table? She particularly loved seeing mothers with their children. It wouldn't bring her own mum back, but whenever she saw a real family, just for a moment she felt like she was part of one. Perhaps watching so many families over the years had developed her spy skills.

Boss was an excellent scout; his wet, black nose to the wind.

'Do you often paddle with your dog?' a voice called out to her. Boss barked in reply, almost like he had understood. He was an extremely intuitive Westie when he wanted to be.

Frankie scanned the shore in the dying light. She saw her new neighbour, JJ, sitting on a boat ramp, feet dangling over the edge.

'Do you often spy on people?' asked Frankie – a classic counter-attack.

JJ laughed. Frankie was glad it was almost dark. He wouldn't have seen how red she went. Even though she was working on her spy skills, she couldn't seem to escape her new neighbour.

'Where did you move from again?' asked Frankie as she paddled closer to him.

'Iceland,' said JJ. 'I lived here on Griffin Close until I was four. My mum says we used to play together when we were really little. Our mums —'

'That was a long time ago,' Frankie cut in. She didn't like this strange boy knowing more about her mum than she did! But at the same time, she wanted to know more. In some way, she felt that JJ could help her unlock the truth about her mother.

'Maybe we could paddle together some time,' JJ said. 'I'm a bit rusty, but we have spare kayaks.' He gestured to his family's own boathouse.

'Okay,' Frankie agreed. It would give her time to uncover further secrets about her new neighbours and, perhaps, her mother. 'How about tomorrow? Same time, same place?'

'Deal,' said JJ.

Frankie waved and pushed out again into the harbour, trying not to think of the past. She stared into the sea fog. It might be too tough to get to the island now that it was getting dark. The thud of a ferry motor drifted across the bay, and ropes clanged on nearby yachts. As she and Boss contemplated the journey, a flash of bright light under the surface caught her eye. A sudden thrill passed through her, laced with fear. Frankie waited a few minutes, peering into the gloom below. There it was again! Another bright light shot below the surface. Could it be a sea creature, or was it man made? Midget submarines had made it into Harbour City in World War II, but she didn't think the lights could be caused by them.

Frankie didn't see or hear the other kayak coming at her until it was almost too late. Its sleek, dark, fibreglass hull sliced through the water soundlessly.

Boss barked as the boat got closer. The kayaks were going to collide! At the last minute, Frankie dug her oar in, swerving to avoid being hit and changing the direction of her kayak.

'Watch out!' she cried. Frankie's kayak spun wildly, wobbling in the water. It was a miracle she and Boss hadn't tipped upside down.

The other kayaker didn't stop, but Frankie was worried. It seemed as though she had tried to capsize them on purpose! Frankie noted the woman's blue eyes and the wisps of brown hair tucked under her baseball cap as they passed each other. The woman had glared at her. Boss continued to growl at the kayak even though it was already metres from them.

'She tried to topple us!' Frankie said to Boss.

'Woof!' Boss agreed. Frankie gave him a pat while trying to hold on the oar steady. They were at a dangerous point in the harbour, where the currents became swift and fast moving. It was a long swim to the shore. Frankie shivered. Her father would be angry if he knew she was out here. Especially as it wasn't safe. Frankie turned to look for the woman in the killer kayak. But she was gone, almost as if she'd never been there. Spooked, Frankie turned her paddle and headed for home.

CHAPTER FIVE

Dead drops are post-office boxes, garbage bins or other places where spies put information for fellow spies to find. This way, information can be shared without agents ever having to meet.

THE SPY'S HANDBOOK

GRIFFIN HOUSE, GRIFFIN CLOSE, HARBOUR CITY
▼

Hanna was dishing up dinner when Frankie slid into her spot at the dining table. 'Sorry I'm late,' said Frankie. 'Are we having schnitzel?' she sniffed the delicious smells wafting out of the kitchen.

'Where were you?' Hanna asked. Frankie could tell she was annoyed. 'I buzzed down, but you didn't answer. I can't come down that often, Frankie,' Hanna complained. 'My knees just aren't up to it.'

Frankie mumbled an excuse. She felt bad for being so late.

'Your dad called,' Hanna said.

'What did he want?' Frankie asked.

'To say goodnight,' said Hanna. 'He's stuck on the Fortress for the next few days, and he may not see you.'

'Typical,' Frankie said, switching on the TV. There he was, on the *Nightly National News*. Fergus Fox was so fit that the prime minister looked old and flabby by comparison. They showed him shaking the prime minister's hand. The newsreader kept saying the words 'top secret' and 'national security project' over and over.

'I wonder what Dad's working on this time?' Frankie mused.

'Probably doing the world some good – like fighting the Alliance,' Hanna said firmly. She was keenly watching the news bulletin.

After dinner, Hanna sent Frankie off to bed with a mug of hot chocolate. On her way down to the boathouse, Frankie paused by her father's study. It was a place she never went into, but tonight curiosity got the better of her. Fuelled by the 'top secret' talk on TV, she opened the door.

The office was white and clean and reminded Frankie of the dentist's surgery. Three large tablet computers sat propped on the desk. Not a single stray piece of paper or crumpled Post-it note disrupted the space. Frankie padded across the room, her heart lurching as the computers clicked on by themselves. She had the feeling that she was being watched, but a quick glance told her there were no cameras in here, not in view, anyway. Numerals scrolled down the computer screens so fast that Frankie couldn't make any meaning of the numbers or pick up any patterns. The information kept coming until the machines stopped suddenly. Frankie reached out to touch the middle screen and knocked over a caddy of pens.

A government seal flashed across the screen. Then, so quickly she almost thought it hadn't happened, a more old-fashioned sort of seal with a dragon-type crest flashed across the screen. But it wasn't a dragon. It was a griffin, just like the one near the front gate. Frankie felt shivers run down her spine, her spy sense on full alert. Frankie lived in a house called Griffin on a street called Griffin Close. *There are just too many coincidences,* thought Frankie. She crouched to pick the pens off the floor.

The door to the office swung open. From her position on the floor, Frankie could see Hanna's slippered feet. Frankie froze. Her spy sense told her to wait and see what happened next. Her housekeeper never came downstairs at night.

From the doorway, Hanna looked and waited, her eyes narrowing when she saw the mug of hot chocolate. She was sure she'd heard someone creeping around Fergus's office. *What is Frankie doing here*? thought Hanna. She waited a good three minutes until she finally closed the door and left. Frankie let go of her breath and felt sweat dripping down her neck.

Frankie heard Hanna's feet shuffling towards her room, then scrambled out of the office as fast as possible. She flew down the cliff stairs in record time. Her heart thumped. For the first time, the still night air and the slow sound of the water lapping at the motorboat outside didn't console her. It frightened her.

Frankie grabbed *The Spy's Handbook* and lugged it into bed. As she got comfortable, nestling the book into the crook between her lap and her doona, the front cover fell open and the strange message swam in front of her eyes. She had no idea how to begin decoding it. Eventually, she gave up and settled into the growing dark of the boathouse. Boss's warmth at her feet made her feel cosy and safe. But then Frankie bolted upright. There was some connection between the events of the day. The woman in the kayak had reminded Frankie of her new bus driver. *They weren't just similar – they were the same person!*

Frankie found it hard to sleep that night. There was no doubt about it, the mystery woman had her spooked.

CHAPTER SIX

A spy agency is like a family. Everyone is a valued member and has their part to play. Children and young people can be brought into an agency for special work that requires special skills. Never underestimate the power, energy and skill of a young person. They act on instinct, and that instinct is usually right. They are essential to any mission.

THE SPY'S HANDBOOK

GRIFFIN HOUSE, GRIFFIN CLOSE, HARBOUR CITY
▼

'Ever had gastro? Worst feeling of my life. Don't know what came over me yesterday!' Frankie's regular bus driver was back the next morning, nattering on.

She had avoided Hanna, slipping off to school before her housekeeper made breakfast. Frankie moved down the bus to avoid the driver sharing any more gory details. She had been hoping to see the female bus driver to work out if she really was the same woman as the kayaker. She was also hoping JJ was on the bus, but there was no sign of him.

'Frankie!' a voice called to her from the back. Rani's black bobbed hair bounced in the sun.

'I'm so glad to see you,' said Frankie, squeezing in next to her friend. There were a million things on Frankie's mind – *The Spy's Handbook*'s coded message, the strange woman in the kayak, and her new friend JJ – but because she was a spy-in-training, she said nothing about any of them.

'How's netball going?' Frankie asked instead. The bus ride continued on in the same way. Rani told her the play-by-plays of last week's netball game, and Frankie tried not to worry about all the strange things that were happening.

'What about you?' Rani asked.

'Um, well ... I know this will sound a bit weird.' Frankie knew she had to give her best friend at least a hint about what was going on. 'Strange things have been happening to me,' she confessed.

'Stranger than defusing a bomb in science class?' Rani asked, her eyebrows raised.

'Yes,' Frankie said. 'I think someone's watching me.'

'That's definitely weird,' Rani said. 'Tell me more.'

So Frankie told her bit by bit about the weird goings-on, from the strange people she'd seen, to meeting JJ and learning more about her mother. She was just about to tell her about *The Spy's Handbook* when they got to school.

Sharing her problems had made Frankie feel a bit better. She would tell Rani everything else later.

•

Frankie left the boathouse that evening, laying a trap behind her. *The Spy's Handbook* had suggested that leaving a hair across the pages of a book was a sure-fire way to discover if someone was reading your stuff. So Frankie stuck a fine strand of hair across the door handle on her way out. An intruder may not see it, but she would know it was there.

JJ was waiting for her in a black fibreglass kayak of his own. Boss squeezed into Frankie's kayak behind her; there was barely any room for the both of them.

'Hey, Boss,' said JJ, reaching over to rub the Westie behind the ears.

'You weren't on the bus today.'

'Gaming tournament,' JJ explained. '*Military Ops*. Mum and Dad sometimes let me stay home to play.'

'Really?' Frankie couldn't believe it. Most parents wanted to get rid of the game. It was addictive. It was also the most popular online game in the world. Frankie had played it once or twice at Rani's. It wasn't as gory as other games – *Military Ops* not only required stamina and skill in shooting, it trained you in covert manoeuvres like remaining hidden from the enemy and how to be strategic. You had to escape tough situations. Mostly, it taught you how to think fast in a dangerous situation.

'You must be pretty good if they let you do that.'

'Not bad,' JJ admitted. 'But this guy called Eddie from Wisconsin beats me every time. Anyway, where are we headed, Captain?'

'Fortress Island,' Frankie said, testing him. 'My dad works there.'

'Let's go and see the famous Fergus Fox.'

Frankie groaned. Did everyone know who her father was?

It was a busy night on the harbour. Frankie looked anxiously for the bus driver/kayaker, but there was no sign of her. Their paddles pulled through the black water, making barely a sound. Tonight, party boats strung with fairy lights and pumping loud music cut across the water.

Fortress Island loomed ahead of them. They left the calm of the bay and headed out onto open water.

As they drew closer to the Fortress, lights shot around them, deep underneath the surface.

'Not again!' Frankie cried, anxiously peering into the dark for movement. Boss barked at the lights, trying to stick his head right into the water.

'What are they?' JJ's voice was almost drowned out by the rising wind. Frankie and JJ stopped paddling to look at the light show. Dark, ominous shapes moved in the water. Small waves slapped at the sides of their boats. Below them, the lights faded in and out.

'No idea! Hurry!' The two chopped through the water. Frankie tried not to panic. She could see the steady curve of the Inner City Bridge ahead of her, and the outline of the parkland at the point. Off to her right was another small island. As long as she didn't look down, everything would be alright. Inside though, a thrill of excitement flashed through her. What had they stumbled upon?

The outer battlement of Fortress Island finally loomed ahead. The pulsing lights began to die away. Her own private playground looked different at night. Frankie wondered if her father was in his lab on the other side of the island.

JJ banked his kayak on the hard stones of the slipway. 'Those lights were pretty weird . . .' he began, trailing off as the night air suddenly came alive. Voices came from the dark. Torchlight swept over the slipway, seeking them out. Why was anyone still here at this time of night? Instinct forced her further into the shadows.

'Get down!' Frankie whispered. Frankie pulled Boss's furry body against her on the wall, his panting breath hot on her face. The voices got louder. Frankie yanked JJ into a small cavity against the slippery wall and they slowed their breathing, forcing themselves to be quiet. Boss started to growl.

A short burst of static crackled through the air.

'Unit one, this is unit two. We're in place at the slipway. They're not here,' grunted a deep male voice nearby, talking into a walkie-talkie. Footsteps crunched on the rock of the breakwater wall above them, loosening small stones.

Frankie and JJ sneaked a look upwards and saw uniformed men speaking in low voices. They shrank back and clenched their eyes shut, expecting to be discovered at any moment. Finally, they heard the men run off at a clip.

'Frankie?' JJ shook her shoulder. 'Were they what I think they were?'

CHAPTER SEVEN

Beginner spies operate on their own; master spies work for an agency, organisation or government. Sometimes these agencies are so covert that they are unknown by all but a select few. For instance, Australia has three secret intelligence organisations, each more covert than the last. Most people, when asked, could only name one.

THE SPY'S HANDBOOK

FORTRESS ISLAND, HARBOUR CITY

▼

'Soldiers,' Frankie gulped. What would *The Spy's Handbook* recommend? She knew she had to take action. First, they needed to find her father. She was really worried about him now. Frankie ignored the brooding night skyline. The harsh lines of industrial machinery, monstrous cranes and towering brick pits looked like angry dinosaurs in the dark, but she *knew* this place. She could rely on her instincts. Fergus Fox's lab was in a warehouse on the other side of Fortress Island. Frankie knew there was only one way to get there in a hurry.

'We'll go through the tunnels!' Frankie was sure of her plan. She pointed to the middle of the island. Lots of passageways ran under it. They had been carved right through the rock, built for emergencies in wartime. JJ nodded uncertainly, but he fell in line behind Frankie.

They crept towards the first entrance, their eyes adjusting to the dim light. Not a sound came out. Boss kept at their side, not keen to go forward without them. Hurricane lamps lit the old-fashioned hazard signs that remained after the World War II air raids. They peered down the tunnel entrance. Frankie's eyes followed the lights on the cavern walls until they disappeared around a bend.

'Go on, Boss!' Frankie whispered. 'Check it out!' The dog ran ahead, disappearing around the corner.

After a few tense minutes, Boss didn't return, so they ran, their feet squelching from the water. Finally, they heard the jangle of his collar. Boss had stopped, frozen, ahead on the path. The fur on the back of his neck had risen, a low growl in his throat.

'What's up, boy?' Frankie murmured, catching up to him and slipping her hand underneath his collar.

Then, as if someone had snapped on a switch, bright lights blinded them and a thundering noise descended. Boss howled and Frankie covered her ears. He took off towards the light, barking.

'Come back, Boss!' JJ yelled, but it was no good.

The booming sound cranked up another hundred decibels, as if a plane were landing on the tunnel roof. A surge of wind screamed down the tunnel, hitting them in the face. JJ turned and saw soldiers running towards them.

'RUN!' he roared. The soldiers were gaining on them. Together, they sprinted towards the other end of the tunnel, grabbing hands, running towards the commotion outside. *We're going to make it,* thought Frankie. *Dad will make everything alright. I'm sure he's nearby.*

JJ tumbled forward, losing his footing and his grip on Frankie's hand. Frankie ran towards Boss and Boss ran towards the unnatural light. She didn't look back. But at the edge of the tunnel, Frankie stopped. A military helicopter lifted off from the ground. At close range, the noise was deafening. She shrieked. Grit stung her

eyes. Soldiers ran towards the chopper, firing at it. Wind whipped her face and her clothes stung against her body.

The helicopter turned so its cockpit faced towards her. Frankie squinted into its dim cabin. The pilot's face was obscured by a flight helmet. Behind him, two dark figures loomed. A man pushed the other up against the window. They were fighting. One man was clearly trying to escape, pulling open the doors. Even if he jumped out at this height, he wouldn't be hurt. He suddenly froze. Frankie saw that the other man was holding a gun as the helicopter began to rise. Then the unarmed man looked directly at Frankie. *Dad?* It was a split-second recognition, before the helicopter turned and lifted in the air, the soldiers firing desperately at it.

'Don't shoot!' she cried, and the shadow of a soldier loomed across her path. Frankie suddenly felt heavy, as though lead had been poured into her. The last thing she saw before she fainted was a set of angry eyes peering out from a yellow beret.

CHAPTER EIGHT

SECURE INTERVIEW ROOM, GROUND LEVEL, FORTRESS ISLAND, HARBOUR CITY

▼

The smell of something disgusting, mixed with a sharp chemical sting, forced Frankie's eyes open. She tried to swallow but her throat was dry and scratchy. For some reason, her pinky finger felt like it was on fire.

'My leg *kills,*' JJ said from nearby, rubbing his thigh. *Phew. He's alive. We're together*, thought Frankie. There was no sign at all of Boss. Frankie tried not to panic.

The soldier with the angry eyes fixed his gaze on them. A bright yellow beret was jammed on his head. A small gold badge was pinned to the side of the beret, the way prefects at Chumsworth pinned their badges to their school blazers. He looked like he could run a thousand miles, bench press a car, and tackle a shark barehanded before breakfast.

'How long have we been here?' asked Frankie.

The soldier glanced at his watch.

'A few hours,' he said.

'What have you done to Boss?' Frankie demanded, her voice cracking.

'Who's your boss?' The soldier leapt up, angry enough to frighten them both with his expression alone. 'Tell me right now,' he demanded.

'He's my dog,' Frankie said.

The soldier frowned, but looked relieved. 'Oh. He's been taken care of,' he said.

Frankie went ballistic. 'You KILLED my dog?'

'Of course not,' said the soldier. 'He's far too valuable for that. He's been taken to the Elite Canine Training Unit.'

Frankie opened her mouth to speak but found that she couldn't form just one question.

'I saw my father,' she said finally.

'The Alliance has him,' said the soldier matter-of-factly.

Next to her, JJ laughed hysterically. 'The Alliance? We're being pranked, right?'

'And we need your help to get him back,' the soldier continued calmly. He pulled a small device from his top pocket, unrolling the screen flat and consulting it. Frankie and JJ couldn't take their eyes off it. It was small and silver, with a see-through screen. Lights blinked across the device, and then a small face appeared to be looking directly up at the soldier.

'What is that?' JJ breathed, but the soldier took no notice of him.

'Copy that. Both of them appear awake and alert,' the soldier muttered. Frankie didn't feel alert. Next her her, JJ looked exhausted. The soldier put the device down, stood, and in a swift move, saluted Frankie and JJ.

'In these difficult circumstances it is my grim duty to officially inform you both that you are being brought out of sleeper status. Active duty commences at 0200,' the soldier said to them. Frankie's stomach turned.

JJ snorted violently. Frankie froze.

'Who are you?' she croaked.

'Captain Benjamin Tucker.'

'I think you've made some kind of mistake . . . er . . . Captain,' JJ spoke quickly. 'We don't work for the army.'

'Neither do I, Agent,' the soldier replied. 'We all work for Griffin.'

Frankie's eyes darted back to the small gold badge on his beret. She saw now that it was a griffin – just like the sandstone carving that guarded her house!

•

At precisely 0200, Frankie, JJ and the captain were on the move. They were chaperoned by soldiers in khaki uniforms. Frankie walked slowly, her legs aching from the sprint through the tunnel.

'Is it time to take them below, sir?' a soldier asked.

'Take a seat in the airlock,' Captain Tucker said to Frankie and JJ, ushering them through a set of steel doors. 'Descent takes approximately three minutes. Your ears will pop.' The Captain punched numbers into a keyboard and a flat screen briefly flared on the wall. Again, the Griffin seal that Frankie had seen in her father's office flitted across the screen.

The small chamber pulsed with a strange heat and a whumping sound. The Captain's eyes were closed. He didn't flinch.

Captain Tucker cracked his eyes open, his icy blue orbs pinning Frankie's. She held his gaze. Tucker rose and keyed in more numbers on the pad and Frankie's stomach jumped, and her ears popped.

'Compression takes place when you dive,' Tucker said.

'We're not diving,' JJ said, pointing at the four walls.

'We are, but without the water,' Tucker said. 'We are descending 100 metres below sea level. The gas in your body has now been compressed.' JJ tried not to chuckle and Frankie nudged him in the ribs.

'Don't make me laugh,' said Frankie.

'Down we go again,' he said. 'You may feel a strange sensation.' Frankie and JJ clutched the bench seats and their stomachs dropped. Finally, the small room stilled and the wall opposite slid open. A huge room, as big as an aircraft hangar, bustled with activity in front of them. Hundreds of soldiers were hard at work hunched over computers. People caught sight of the three of them standing there, and gradually the frenzy of activity stopped and a hush fell over the huge space. There was a bark, and a small white fur ball bounded towards Frankie.

'Agents Fox and Jensen,' said Captain Tucker. 'Welcome to Mission Icefall.'

CHAPTER NINE

Animals can be recruited as intelligence officers. Dolphins, certain species of birds, as well as ordinary pets can be trained for espionage.

THE SPY'S HANDBOOK

COMMAND CENTRE, LEVEL 30, GRIFFIN HQ

▼

'Boss!' Frankie cried, spotting the little white dog. Boss leapt up into her arms, licking her, his collar jangling against her wrist. He had a new collar and tags. The faint imprint of a griffin on his new tag caught the light. Flipping it over, Frankie saw it had been engraved with *ECTU – Elite Canine Training Unit*. A young man approached her with a lead, handing it to Frankie. 'One of the best elite canines I've ever come across,' the soldier said. 'You've trained him well.' Frankie raised her eyebrows. She had a hard time telling Boss to get off her bed, let alone training him!

She looked at Boss's sweet white face, his black eyes brimming with intelligence, his short white coat looking bright and shiny. She dropped her head to his, smelling his clean fur and holding him close. Boss was family. As she watched his devoted eyes gazing up at her, she felt proud that he made a pretty good spy, too.

On one hangar wall, a large symbol of a griffin looked down on them. It was fierce, its large hooked beak thrusting upwards, its wings in full flight. The strong legs and tail of a lion made it an awe-inspiring creature. It was the same image as the one she had seen on her father's computer. It was the same beast as the one on her driveway.

She hadn't been dreaming. She hadn't been imagining things. All the clues of the last few months had added up to something. Her spy senses had actually detected that she was involved with this Griffin organisation – whatever it was.

A tall, important-looking officer in khaki marched towards them and saluted. Her yellow beret was rolled up and secured under the epaulette on her shoulder. She nodded briefly at Captain Tucker, who returned the salute.

Her dark brown bob was tucked behind her ears, her eyes almost black and piercing. She clearly meant business.

'Commander,' Tucker said, and she nodded.

'Agent Fox, we meet again,' the woman said, looking seriously at Frankie. 'Last time you were just a baby.' She turned to JJ. 'Agent Jensen, you've grown, too, since I last saw you in Iceland.'

'Really?' JJ asked. How could this stranger have seen him before? This was way too weird.

'Your Under-10s football final at Laugardalur valley field in Reykjavik.' JJ's mouth opened and closed, but nothing came out. 'You lost 2–0 against the Falcons, as I recall.'

'Not my finest match,' JJ muttered.

'Where are we?' Frankie cut in.

'And who are you?' JJ added.

'I am Commander of this mission. We are at the headquarters of Griffin, the international spy agency. We protect the world's greatest treasure: freedom.' She paused to let Frankie and JJ take in this major piece of information. 'Most importantly, we fight the Alliance.'

Here we are at Griffin, Frankie thought. *Just fighting for the world's freedom. We're going to shut the Alliance down! Just the usual. Saving the world.*

'Why griffins?' JJ asked.

'Because griffins were known to guard and protect, and that is what our agents do,' the woman said. 'The world needs us more now than ever before.' She looked deadly serious. Her hand clenched into a fist at her side. 'The Alliance will never defeat us!'

Frankie stole a look at JJ. That was intense!

They detoured across the hangar to another set of steel doors, to a conference room. 'MISSION BRIEFING ROOM', the sign on the door read. Frankie and JJ sat at the table, across from the Commander and Captain Tucker. Boss leapt up onto Frankie's lap.

'This emergency briefing for Mission Icefall is called to order —' the Commander consulted the large diving watch on her wrist '— at 0217. The situation is grave. Agent Fox, senior, has been taken by the Alliance. Tonight, Griffin came under attack on home soil. We must find him and bring him back. Alive.'

'Can't the prime minister help?' Frankie asked, thinking about when she saw her dad on TV.

'I'm afraid not,' said Captain Tucker. 'She doesn't actually know that Griffin exists. It's too top-secret, even for her. Your father knows her from his work, but she has no idea he is a secret agent. We're going to have to save him ourselves.'

'I know I can help,' Frankie said confidently. 'I've been in training for a while now.'

The Commander and Captain Tucker looked at her. 'You mean you *knew* about Griffin?' Frankie's hands shook slightly. She clasped them together, hoping no one would notice.

'Oh, no,' said Frankie hastily. 'It's just that there were all sorts of clues. They make sense now.' She hoped she looked more confident than she sounded.

Captain Tucker raised an eyebrow. 'Well, we knew you were a great agent, Fox, but I must say you have a sixth sense for spying.' He looked at her the way Miss Porter had looked at her after she'd defused that bomb in science class.

'I specialise in code-cracking,' she said. 'Cryptology. That sort of thing.'

The Commander cleared her throat and wiped something from her eye. Was she crying? Frankie looked at her curiously.

'Agent Fergus Fox was working on something so important, it is no wonder they kidnapped him!' The Commander hammered her fist on the table and Frankie jumped in her seat. 'They stole him from under our nose,' she roared.

'So how do we get him back?' Frankie asked.

'It's not that easy,' Captain Tucker said. 'Our first priority is to protect Icefall. Your father is the only one that knows the secret to the technology. Most likely they will turn to what they do best – brainwashing. Our sources have reason to believe they've created a truth serum.'

'We've got to go after them and find him! Now!' Frankie said. She banged her fist on the table, just like the Commander, but it didn't have quite the same impact.

'Your father is a brilliant scientist,' the Commander said to Frankie. 'He has invented a technology so new, so powerful, that it could change the world. It uses energy waves to bring frozen waterfalls – or icefalls – to life. In the wrong hands, this technology could completely destroy the world's frozen tundra – Antarctica, the Arctic Circle, Greenland, the Himalayas . . .' The Commander paused.

'But in the right hands, the potential for harnessing that energy is incredible,' Captain Tucker took over the explanation. 'It would work just like solar energy – it is a completely green energy source.'

'But you're not going to do anything to save him?' Frankie asked again.

Captain Tucker looked her straight in the eye. 'Of course we will. We already have a rescue team out scanning for him. The Alliance will play with him until they have what they want. But we will find him before then. And we need Icefall.'

'Is it on file somewhere?' JJ asked.

'You don't know my father,' Frankie muttered.

'Agent Fox, senior, never kept all his information in one place. He was right to be suspicious – the Alliance has spies everywhere,' said Tucker. 'We have his research here at Griffin for the Icefall technology, but the trigger key is hidden.'

'Trigger key?' asked JJ.

'It's like the bullet in a gun. The last part of the technology that makes it *work*. The thing that actually unlocks the energy trapped inside glaciers.'

'But is it a *key*?' Frankie asked. Her father could have put a key anywhere.

'It's a device very similar to a USB drive,' Tucker explained. 'The "key" to making this all work, has been hidden by your father. It's the final link in the code that will activate Icefall.'

'I can check his office. Turn the house upside down?' Frankie suggested.

'That would be a waste of your spying skills,' the Commander said. 'Your father has mentioned your gifts for code-cracking to us on a number of occasions now,' she said. 'He said you were a genius. And he wouldn't just leave it lying around.'

Genius? Her father had called her a genius? A warm glow spread in Frankie's chest.

The Commander continued. 'We suspect he may have left clues that will lead us to the key – if we can crack them.'

The fuzzy feeling disappeared when Frankie thought of her father being held captive and brainwashed by the Alliance . . . and the Icefall technology falling into the wrong hands.

No. It would not happen. She would help Griffin to find the trigger key – wherever it was – and get her father back.

'I will do whatever I can,' Frankie said. Beside her, Boss barked like he understood.

'Your father encrypted his work to protect himself,' Tucker said.

'Sounds like Dad,' said Frankie.

'If the Alliance gets their hands on this technology, the world will be far worse off,' spluttered the Commander. 'We must attack and —'

'Counter-attack,' finished Frankie.

Tucker opened a folder and pushed some pictures towards Frankie and JJ. A grainy photo of a woman with thick brown hair, a pinched nose and blue eyes flashed before them.

'My bus driver!' Frankie exclaimed.

'Are you sure?' asked Tucker.

'Yes, she tried to capsize me.'

'In a bus?' Tucked looked confused.

'No, in a kayak,' Frankie said.

Tucker's pen stopped and he looked at Frankie curiously.

'Her name is Mirka Blak. She has obviously been gathering intelligence on you,' he confirmed.

'We captured her last night. She is a five-star operative for the Alliance. Trained in mixed martial arts. World-champion kick boxer. Top-flight ninjitsu. Accomplished scuba diver. Speaks five languages. She is considered highly dangerous.'

The Commander's face paled. 'We need you both more than ever,' she said to Frankie and JJ. 'You both have the highest security clearance. At your families' requests, you weren't supposed to be brought out of sleeper status until aged 16. But we need you now.'

Tucker slid more photos over the table to them. There were childhood photos of Frankie and her parents. There were baby pictures of JJ and more recent pictures of him hiking across the icy wilderness of what Frankie guessed was Iceland.

'We've been watching you for a long time,' Tucker explained.

'Have you bugged my bedroom?' Frankie blurted out. 'Someone's been touching my stuff.'

The Commander raised an eyebrow.

Tucker shook his head. 'No,' he said emphatically. 'Not us.'

'Could be the Alliance,' the Commander said. 'Be very, very careful.' A cold chill went through Frankie.

To think that an Alliance agent's hands had been on her stuff . . . had the dangerous Mirka Blak been in her room?

The next photo showed a fit-looking couple standing in wetsuits. 'Mum and Dad!' said JJ.

'Agents Jensen, senior,' Captain Tucker said. 'Retired.'

A photo of Frankie's parents in the days when she was just a baby was next. 'This is where everything went wrong and we lost Agent Joanna Fox,' said the Commander gravely. 'It's time you learned about Mission Avalanche.'

The Commander began to tell the story . . .

CHAPTER TEN

A spy on their own is just one part of the puzzle.
They are just one cog in the wheel of a big operation.

THE SPY'S HANDBOOK

CHOMO LONZO MOUNTAIN PASS, NEPAL — ELEVEN YEARS EARLIER
▼

The Kangshung valley is in a cold, windswept mountain range in the Himalayas of Nepal. No one goes there unless they have to.

It is very near Makalu, the fifth-highest mountain peak in the world. Some say the Kangshung valley looks like the wings of an outstretched eagle. In the shadow of these mountains, in the narrow Chomo Lonzo pass, lies a monastery that housed monks for generations. Their prayers and incantations fell like kisses on the rugged mountains and the bleak valleys below.

But the monks packed their bags years ago. Their former home, which clings to the side of a mountain the way a barnacle clings to a whale, became a small inn with only one room for hire. The Inn of a Thousand Joys is a destination for the hardiest of souls, those daredevil mountaineers and adventurers. It is decrepit and bare. Swallows nest in its crumbling roof.

So when a tall man with dark wavy hair and a woman with hair as white as snow stood at the counter in the

Inn of a Thousand Joys, Mr Lo, the innkeeper, took a deep breath. He rubbed the fine silver necklace with its eagles' wings around his neck. It had brought him nothing but good luck and protection his whole life. It had been handed down by his grandparents and great-grandparents and probably for hundreds of years before that. These people before him were mysterious; for some reason the hairs on his neck rose.

Mr Lo was surprised to see that the woman held a little cherub with a mop of white-blonde curls, wrapped up in a brightly coloured rug held close to her rosy cheek. Children were a rare sight in the valley. Mr Lo wondered why anyone would bring a child to such an isolated and eerie place.

He led the family to their room at to the top of the rickety stairs of the inn and handed them the iron key. The baby looked at him, her brown eyes seeing all the way into his soul. Mr Lo breathed deeply. The child had asked for the necklace, he was sure of it. The baby needed his pendant. He reached around his neck, taking off the silver necklace, and slipped it over the baby's head without a second thought.

'For protection,' he said to the man and the woman. Their eyes widened but they said nothing, only nodding their thanks. As he descended the stairs, Mr Lo whispered a small prayer to keep them and himself protected. He could see danger ahead. This family was not safe, he feared.

The room for hire was sparse, the rolled mattress on the floor the only piece of furniture. It was lumpy and hard. Out of the window, a breeze whistled through the mountain pass, and prayer flags whipped in the late summer winds. The Alliance lab that they had come to destroy was hidden somewhere in the valley.

The husband and wife put their rucksacks on the wooden floor. It had taken weeks on foot to reach Chomo Lonzo, and they had done their best to avoid arousing suspicion. They had travelled through Nepal with their bags on their backs, always watching to see if they were being followed, always hoping to remain undetected. Their baby was part of their cover. Everyone they met along the road thought they were just a family with an appetite for adventure. What those strangers didn't know was that they were a family on a dangerous mission.

The man pulled the woman into a tight embrace. 'The job ahead is not easy,' he whispered, looking tenderly at his wife and baby. 'But the world needs us. The Alliance must be broken.'

His wife swept away a tear. 'I know,' she said. 'It must be done.' Together, they looked at their child. She gurgled back at them, her rosebud lips almost smiling.

They waited for night to fall, leaving a neat stack of money for Mr Lo. They would never see the old man again. In the cloak of darkness, they hooked their abseiling gear on and rappelled right out of the window, onto the valley floor below. It was their only way to reach the Alliance, to destroy their laboratory. The baby was nestled in a sling at her mother's waist.

The mother went first. She was a skilled rock climber. Her husband was a brilliant scientist as well as a trained agent and he had mixed the explosives himself, ready to detonate when they reached the Alliance's secret lab. A lab that was being used to make a virus so powerful it could make whole countries sick.

Once they were safe in the valley below, they took off at great speed. They had been training at altitude for months, their lungs adjusting to the thin air of the Himalayas. They hacked their way across scrubby bush, rocky paths and ground that had turned to mud from the fallen dew. It got colder the higher they climbed. There was not a sound, and that made the travelling family even more nervous. They began picking their way up a mountain slope, rising above the valley just as the moon did.

'Switching to night vision,' the mother whispered. She fumbled in the dark, placing her goggles over her eyes. As she adjusted to night vision, she saw a flash of body heat.

'Run!' the woman called out to her husband, alerting him to the presence of the enemy.

An Alliance agent sprang onto the pathway before they could get away. He looked strong and dangerous. His black clothes were the hallmark of the Alliance. A dark cloth mask covered his face, leaving only the gleam of his eyes.

He grabbed at her, but the woman expertly ducked, her hand going round to secure her baby at the front. The father turned to fight, surprising the enemy behind him. The Alliance agent stumbled, wobbled and, for a slow moment, rocked on the edge before falling into the darkness.

Two more dark figures crept up the path behind them, but this time the man was ready for them. He held his bag close as he overpowered the agents. It carried the explosives required to destroy the Alliance laboratory.

The woman scrambled up the path. At the top, three large figures stood, watching and waiting for her. She weighed up her chances. She couldn't save both herself and her baby.

'Swap the packages,' she cried to her husband.

'Now!' He called to her across the mountain path. The mother propelled the baby into the air, her careful aim making sure the child would find the steady hands of her father. He threw the explosives bag through the air, the two precious bundles passing each other.

'Run!' she cried. 'Save yourself!' The father deftly zipped the baby inside his jacket. Then he ran. His wife was smart and tough, and she would find a way to get to the rendezvous point.

'Urgent pick-up, NOW!' he cried into his transmitter, using the emergency frequency. He sparked a flare, the beacon throwing a strange red light on the night around them. He barked coordinates to mission control and ran back down the mountain path, his feet sliding in the mud, veering dangerously close to the edge of the outcrop. Yet he managed to stay upright and ahead of another agent on his tail.

He sprinted through the dark, and got to the clearing just as the Griffin chopper landed. He hauled himself up, handing the baby to his boss. She was strapped into a capsule, the silver charm around her neck shining in the green cockpit light of the helicopter.

The chopper jerked into the air. 'No!' cried the father, gripping his superior's arm. 'My wife! She'll be here!' His frantic voice rose above the wind.

'Mission complete?' the Commander asked urgently, her dark eyes searching his. The agent shook his head.

'Two minutes!' the Commander said. The chopper hovered off the ground, waiting.

But 30 seconds later, an ominous sound rang out from the Kangshung valley. The blast of a bomb sideswiped the chopper.

'NOOOOOOOO!' the man cried. His wife had the explosives . . . that could only mean one thing. She couldn't have got away in time. The baby started to sob, and Fergus Fox held his daughter's hand tightly as tears dripped down his face.

CHAPTER ELEVEN

Intelligence must be gathered and decoded. New intelligence falling into the wrong hands can be a disaster and the role of the spy is to stay one step ahead of rival agencies.

THE SPY'S HANDBOOK

COMMAND CENTRE, LEVEL 30, GRIFFIN HQ
▼

Frankie's necklace burned at her throat like it was on fire. Jumbled images of the imagined Mr Lo, the unforgiving cliffs of Chomo Lonzo, and the fear her mother must have felt ran through in her mind. Why had her father never told her any of this?

'There was nothing we could do,' the Commander said. 'We had to fly back to base and get you safe.'

JJ glanced at Frankie's shocked face. 'It's going to be okay,' he whispered, his grey eyes shining. 'We're in this together.' She smiled at JJ. It was good to have a friend here.

'We're due in the Prep Tank,' Captain Tucker said, looking at his watch and beckoning Fox and Jensen.

'Commander, thank you,' the officers saluted each other.

'Goodbye, Frankie,' the Commander said. Frankie, JJ and Captain Tucker went to another set of steel doors, and this time they rose a few floors. When the doors opened, their eyes had to adjust to the darkness.

In front of them was what looked like the world's largest fish tank. Frankie and JJ stared at the enormous pool. Instead of orcas and dolphins gliding through the water, soldiers in scuba gear darted around on machines so fast they could barely make them out.

'We know you're both exceptionally strong rowers and swimmers,' said Tucker. 'That was intentional on our part.'

'I've always come first in swimming carnivals,' JJ admitted.

Tucker nodded. 'We had you swimming from very young ages. We trained you both in JJ's pool on Griffin

Close. In fact, Frankie's house was the original Griffin HQ,' he said.

'Griffin agents seem to have a thing for the water,' a familiar voice said. Frankie swivelled. A woman in a wetsuit was striding towards them. Her black hair was slicked back and her eyes shone like sapphires. A small Griffin insignia was stitched on her suit.

'Miss Porter?' Frankie said.

'Most people around here know me as Westwood, Agent Fox.'

'Huh?' asked JJ.

'JJ, meet my science teacher, Miss – I mean, Westwood.'

'There's no time for chit-chat,' Tucker said, looking at Agent Westwood with an uncharacteristic smile. 'I'll leave you to it.' He strode back towards the lift.

Westwood's eyes followed Tucker, and then she turned back to Frankie and JJ. 'I'm so glad that you're finally here,' Agent Westwood smiled warmly at Frankie. She looked at JJ. 'Ready, Agent Jensen?'

He nodded.

'This is where we complete the first stage of aquapod training,' she said. 'This tank is around the size of five Olympic swimming pools. It holds over twelve million litres of water.'

'Why don't you train in the harbour?' asked JJ. 'It's close by.'

'I did see some strange lights under the water . . .' Frankie said.

'Very well observed, Agent Fox. Our agents are on open-water patrol in the harbour right now. In fact, that's how we first knew you were coming.'

CHAPTER TWELVE

Technology is always evolving. Five years into the future, the world will be radically different. Good spies can predict these changes. They love new technologies. Good agencies invent these new technologies.

THE SPY'S HANDBOOK

MARINE PREP TANK, LEVEL 27, GRIFFIN HQ

▼

Frankie and JJ were dressed in custom-made shiny silver wetsuits. Frankie stuffed her curls into the suit's hood. Only their faces and hands were left uncovered. A tingling warmth came from the material. It felt like being wrapped in a doona.

Three aquapods floated on the surface of the pool. Westwood was sitting on the largest one. They were a cross between a jet ski and a motorbike. The black and shiny machines looked menacing in the water, even resting on the surface.

'We built a special pod just for you, Agent Fox,' Westwood said. Frankie's pod had an attachment. Westwood hit a button and the lid of the pillion pod opened up. In it sat Boss, smiling up at Frankie, eager to begin the training session.

Frankie and JJ dived in. 'Aggh! It's freezing!' Frankie spluttered, coming up for air. Together, the two of them swam out to the floating pods. Frankie hauled herself on, her feet instinctively looking for the footholds. Beneath her, the machine seemed powerful ... and dangerous. She patted Boss's muzzle and he gave her an encouraging lick.

'What speeds do these things reach?' JJ asked from the saddle of his aquapod.

'About 80 knots.' said Agent Westwood. Pressing a button on the dash, she said. 'Your helmets and spare air are in the dash.'

Out of her dash rose a sleek black helmet, connected to the aquapod by a hose. 'Breathing apparatus,' Westwood explained. 'You have enough air for thirty minutes.' She fitted it over her head, then revved the handlebars. Waves

fanned out behind the pod and Westwood was off, tearing across the tank at high speed. She disappeared under the water and didn't resurface.

'Here goes nothing!' said JJ. He revved his handlebars and his aquapod flew across the water.

JJ roared off, the waves from his wake making Frankie's pod rock back and forth. He skimmed a partial circuit of the huge tank, returning to Frankie and idling his motor.

'That was AWESOME!' JJ exclaimed, his cheeks bright red. 'Now I'm going under.' He pressed a button on the dash and his breathing helmet extended. He fitted it on his head, gave Frankie the thumbs up and took off again. Frankie watched him skim across the water at top speed. Then suddenly he was gone, with barely a ripple left on the surface.

Frankie leaned over and gave Boss a pat. He licked her hand. She put on her helmet, and closed Boss's pod capsule.

'Ready, Boss?' Frankie murmured, looking through the visor. She didn't feel ready. The Commander's story kept running through her mind. But she had to get her father back and complete the mission. She turned the throttle and the aquapod took off, darting over the water. It felt like flying. Her stomach lurched and she tightened her grip on the handlebars, urging the machine to go faster.

The force of the water nearly pushed her off the aquapod as she went underwater. Her feet held fast in the stirrups and she gripped the handlebars even more tightly. Her visor came alive, lighting up with tracking signals of the other pods in her vision. Westwood's voice was suddenly in her ear. 'Hear me, Agent Fox? Follow us down here; we're on a training circuit.'

She saw JJ ducking and weaving ahead of her, steering the pod to the left and the right. His name flitted across the screen on her visor as soon as she saw him.

Frankie held on and turned the handles even further. The pod responded beneath her. It was just like riding a quad bike, with the gears shifting beneath her. Even as she zoomed along the bottom of the tank, she thought of her father. It made her even more determined to find him.

'Ocean conditions now, team,' Westwood said. 'Follow the small yellow tail-light.' Frankie peered and squinted and finally saw a light ahead. To her right, she saw the faint glow of JJ's pod.

Frankie followed, the nose of the pod slicing through the surface, making her stomach dance with the sudden jump. For a moment the pod was airborne; then it came to rest on the water with a splat, floating with the others. JJ surfaced next to her and they removed their helmets.

'Full marks, agents,' Westwood said, diving off her pod and swimming to the edge of the tank, where Captain Tucker stood.

'Phase two mission training begins now,' he said, arms folded across his Griffin uniform.

Their old clothes had vanished in the change rooms. In their place were new khaki overalls with the small gold Griffin insignia on each chest pocket. Frankie touched her name label fondly. *Agent Fox.* Had her parents worn these exact uniforms?

Frankie swallowed hard. Tears were useless right now. One parent was gone; the other had been kidnapped.

The most important thing right now was to get Agent Fergus Fox back safely and to complete Mission Icefall. And then, maybe Frankie would find out the whole truth about her mother.

CHAPTER THIRTEEN

Each spy has a different role within an organisation. Usually they are suited to their specialties, skills and interests.

THE SPY'S HANDBOOK

TECH UNIT, LEVEL 17, GRIFFIN HQ

▼

For the first time since arriving on Fortress Island, Frankie, Boss and JJ went their separate ways. JJ went to a new floor for Tech training. A young woman with spiky red hair was there to greet him.

'I'm Agent Moss,' she said excitedly. She seemed younger than the other Griffin agents – only a few years older than JJ. 'I've got your desk all set up.' JJ followed her as she weaved in and out of cubicles and workstations. Around them, adults hunched over desks, clattering away at keyboards.

'Do you like coffee or hot chocolate?' she asked.

'Both,' he blurted out. He wasn't technically allowed to drink coffee at home, but he figured Moss didn't need to know that.

'Mocha coming right up,' she said. They rounded a final corner. 'This is mine.' Moss gestured to a messy desk covered in tablets and about five monitors. *Agent Edwina Moss, Tech Unit*, the name badge read. 'Excuse the mess. That's yours,' she said, pointing to a neat, white space.

JJ's desk was pristine and high-tech just the way he liked it. It was almost as though they knew exactly what his desk looked like at home . . .

'We've put a few things here to make you feel comfortable,' Moss said, beaming.

A wall of screens sat facing the empty chair. A super-thin, flexible tablet like the one Captain Tucker had was on the desk. His fingers itched to play with it. A photo of his beloved Tigers footy team was pinned to the cubicle wall. A cricket ball mounted on a plaque hung next to it. He looked more closely.

'Is that signed by the Australian captain?'

Agent Moss nodded.

JJ couldn't believe it. He even had a name badge at the entrance to his cubicle. *Agent James Jensen, Tech Unit.* JJ breathed deeply. He was eleven years old, and he had a job. Possibly the best job on the whole planet!

'Take a seat,' she said. 'I guess I should tell you my other identity. Remember your arch-nemesis from *Military Ops*? Eddie from Wisconsin?'

CHAPTER FOURTEEN

A captured spy is like a caged lion.

THE SPY'S HANDBOOK

ALLIANCE FLOATING BUNKER #1, SOMEWHERE IN THE PACIFIC OCEAN
▼

Agent Fergus Fox groaned and touched his hand to his head. It was pounding. Even worse, he saw that the top of his little finger had a deep cut. The Alliance had obviously found and removed the tracking device Griffin had inserted under his skin back when he had first joined. No wonder Griffin hadn't rescued him yet. He felt sick to his stomach.

Frankie. The last thing he remembered was seeing Frankie's face as the Alliance chopper rose and lifted off Fortress Island. *How could he have been so stupid?*

He had been ambushed. Fergus flexed his hands and sniffed the air. Strangely, he felt no pain, but rather a woozy sense of time passing in the cell around him. The room lurched. He realised that the reason he felt sick was because they were on water. It was quite embarrassing that a top Griffin agent was affected by seasickness. Fergus had managed to hide it for years.

Manacles circled his wrists and he yanked on the chain to see if there was any give. The handcuffs rubbed against his skin. The chain was only long enough for him to reach a tap with running water and a small pail for a toilet. There was no bed, just a rolled up mattress on the ground. Fergus was frustrated. It was almost as if this place had been designed with him in mind – whoever had captured him knew exactly what he was capable of. How was that possible?

In the control room of the Alliance floating bunker, several sets of eyes watched the Griffin agent in the cell. They had been wise not to give this man any chances. They knew he was well-trained in the art of escape.

Footsteps fell across the floor of the cell. Fergus gasped in shock at the figure in front of him.

'Hello, darling,' the ice-cold voice said. 'It's good to see you again.'

CHAPTER FIFTEEN

Don't discard the old ways. Spies use techniques that
have been tried and tested as well as all the latest
high-tech gadgets.

THE SPY'S HANDBOOK

TESTING LAB #1, LEVEL 13, GRIFFIN HQ
▼

Frankie stood at a set of doors marked 'Lab #1'. Tucker
had left her with a swift salute, chasing down some
new intelligence. Ominously, a sign underneath said
'TESTING IN PROGRESS'. Better now than never.
She pushed open one of the flaps and stole a look inside.

But before she could take a step inside, a Griffin
agent appeared.

'Welcome!' the agent said. He was dressed in khaki overalls with the gold Griffin insignia. He had a shiny bald head, a white moustache and little horn-rimmed glasses, which he now peered over.

Frankie felt like a bug under a microscope.

'You look just like both of them,' he said finally, after he'd made his inspection of her.

'Like who?' asked Frankie, confused.

'Your parents, of course,' the man replied, twirling his moustache. 'I'd recognise you anywhere, Frankie Fox. The last time I saw you, you were around six months old, I believe,' he said.

Frankie wondered if she really did look like her mother. Was she going to look just like her when she grew up?

He thrust his hand out. 'Agent Migalowski, at your service,' he said, almost bowing. 'People around here call me Miggles.' He walked over to a nearby bench, grabbed a tape measure and returned to her. He began wrapping it around her head. 'Don't laugh. As much as I love my toys, I'm a great believer in the old ways, too.'

'Now, Frankie, I'm going to give you some very important tools to get you through Mission Icefall,' he said, holding the tape measure across her eyes and nose. 'It is essential that they don't fall into the wrong hands. Wars have been won and lost on the smallest things – some of them instruments of intelligence gathering.'

He finished with the tape measure and crossed the room to a large silver drawer. 'Ah! Here they are!' he said. With a flourish, he turned and presented Frankie with a pouch.

She opened the pouch to find a pair of earrings. 'I don't have pierced ears,' said Frankie. 'Dad won't let me.'

'These are no ordinary earrings,' said Miggles confidently. 'Put them on.'

The tiny silver studs were magnets that she placed on the front and back of her earlobes. Frankie gave the thumbs up. Miggles walked across the lab, out the vinyl

doors and kept walking. She could no longer hear his footsteps. Then came a loud voice.

'Twelve times seven is eighty-four. Twelve times eight is?' Miggles asked.

'Ninety-six,' answered Frankie. It was incredible. He sounded as though he was right next to her.

'The world's most powerful hearing aids,' he said as he walked back into the lab a few moments later. 'Very handy in a situation when you need to hear exactly what's being said a hundred metres away.'

Frankie slipped them off her ears and back into the pouch. These earrings were going to prove *very* useful. She wondered if she could use them at school. They could come in handy. Frankie immediately thought of listening in on her fencing opponent's coach during bouts. Or maybe even overhearing JJ's conversations at home. She shook her head. That would be plain wrong.

Almost as if he had read her mind, Miggles said, 'Just remember, the earrings must be used for the purposes of good, not evil. And now for my latest creation,' said Miggles. He looked very pleased with himself. 'Perfect for tracking someone who you think might be following you, or someone you literally want to keep your eye on.' He brought out a pair of dull black eyeglasses.

'Oh,' said Frankie, a little bit disappointed.

'Slip them on!' Miggles said.

She did so. Nothing. There was nothing exciting about them. Miggles slipped his own pair on and turned to focus on the far wall of the lab.

'See that fire extinguisher?' Miggles asked. Frankie nodded. 'Bet you can't read the serial number at the bottom of the can!' Frankie looked at him dubiously over the glasses.

'Touch the right arm of your glasses.' Frankie's view suddenly zoomed into focus. She was no longer looking at the far wall. Instead, she was looking at the label on the fire extinguisher.

'They're like binoculars!' she said.

'Left arm zooms out,' Miggles confirmed.

'I can read the serial number perfectly from here!' Frankie zoomed out again and the glasses adjusted to normal vision.

'Excellent,' said Miggles.

'Now, for the *pièce de résistance* – you do know what that means?' Miggles asked.

'It's a French phrase first recorded in 1839. It means *the best part*,' Frankie replied.

Miggles was clearly impressed. 'Couldn't have said it better myself.' He handed her a small silver canister. 'This is very, very powerful stuff.'

CHAPTER SIXTEEN

A good spy adapts to new environments and new situations with ease.

' THE SPY'S HANDBOOK

TECH UNIT, LEVEL 17, GRIFFIN HQ
▼

Griffin agent James Jensen hunched over the three devices in his new work cube. JJ's stomach was satisfyingly full. He'd gorged himself on the hot food buffet at the Griffin cafeteria. He had a problem with buffets. He could never just stop at the waffles, the pancakes and the omelettes. He always felt guilty and went back for yoghurt and fruit – as if eating something healthy would cancel out the bad.

'I don't know why Griffin agents aren't fat,' James muttered.

'Our combat training takes care of that. It's a cross between Israel's Krav Maga and taekwondo,' Moss laughed. 'You can basically eat whatever you like.' She patted her stomach.

JJ hoped that training didn't start any time soon. Instead, he focused on the numbers swimming on the screen in front of him.

'Any luck?' Agent Moss asked. 'Anything I've missed?'

James's brow furrowed. There was something about the firewall he was hacking into. It was bugging him. There. A weakness.

'I think I may have found a way into the Alliance's system.'

'How?' asked Moss.

'They're trying to hack into our radar detection shields,' JJ explained. 'But we can intercept their information and use it to attack *them* instead.'

Moss sat down to take a look at his screen. James pointed out a small pattern that seemed to repeat over and over.

'Gotcha,' was all she said.

•

Frankie and Boss were on their way back to Griffin Close, in their aquapod. She'd have to get her kayak, which was at Griffin HQ, later. As they neared home, she shut the engines off. It looked spooky underwater. Old drifts of seaweed caught in the boat ramp and the house above looked wobbly and shimmery. Frankie raised the aquapod up above the surface and pressed a button that lowered the anchor. She flipped up Boss's pillion pod and they both jumped out and ran up the boat ramp.

Frankie rolled her sleeve back and glanced at her watch. *Hanna's probably called the police by now,* she thought.

But looking up at the main house, there was not a peep. Frankie slipped her new glasses on and zoomed in. There were no shadows at the window, no figure at the kitchen. No sign of the police, or anyone at all. She swept up the ramp and peered in the window, not entering the boathouse. Frankie padded around outside. Nothing looked out of place – yet. Boss scouted the perimeter, looking for clues.

Touching her ears, Frankie switched the magnifying audio on to the top of the range. There was nothing – not a sound. No dishes clattering, no whirr of a vacuum cleaner. Together, she and Boss crept slowly up the stairs to the main house. She could search the house and find where her dad had hidden the trigger key.

CHAPTER SEVENTEEN

A spy does what they have to do. Sometimes they have to make tough decisions in the best interests of their country or organisation. It is always for the greater good. That means that a spy can't think about what's best for them – they have to think about what's right for the world.

THE SPY'S HANDBOOK

COMMAND CENTRE, LEVEL 30, GRIFFIN HQ
▼

Agents Moss and Jensen strode through the Command Centre, straight to the briefing room.

'We've got coordinates,' said Agent Moss. 'The Alliance Bunker is floating approximately sixty clicks west of the Mariana Trench, near Guam,' she said.

The Commander's eyes flicked over the information on her tablet. 'Then what are waiting for? Send a rescue unit immediately. And let's get Frankie!'

•

Frankie raced through the house, heading to her father's office. It was empty. Boss stayed close to her side, protecting her every move, his eyes peeled for the enemy. Behind his soft black eyes and adorable white furry face beat the heart of a true Griffin agent.

Frankie paused at the back door and looked down to the boathouse. The funicular was at the top of the stairs. *Think, Frankie! What's your strategy? Where's the trigger key. What could I be looking for? A clue, a location? Or has it been in plain sight all this time? . . .* She pulled the green 'go' lever. The funicular winch began turning and the small elevator began its descent. Frankie's eyes stayed focused on the boathouse. For some reason, her spy sense kept telling her that was the place. If any Alliance agents were hiding there, hopefully the funicular would draw them out.

Nothing stirred, not even the harbour. While the furnicular went down, Frankie stole down the steps, keeping to the shadows. The funicular wheezed to its halt

at the base of the cliff, its doors opening. Time seemed
to slow down. Frankie waited for movement.

'All clear,' she whispered to Boss, as they stole across
to the back of the boathouse.

She ran to the door and glanced at the handle.
The hair was gone! That meant someone had been in
her room.

Inside, Frankie yanked out *The Spy's Handbook*. She
had a gut feeling, an *instinct,* that the answer to where
the trigger key might be within its pages.

She traced the confusing letters once again.

TCITNAL HREHGNE EESESE! STOWOA ELNIFG

She pulled her copy of *Cryptology for Dummies* off her desk. It recommended trying a few types of ciphers, including a reversed alphabet or a half-reversed alphabet. Nothing seemed to work. The message was as complicated as ever.

Frankie swept the book off the table angrily. It tumbled to the floor, falling open at a chapter called 'Block Ciphers'. She peered down. Frustrated, she gave the code one last chance.

Block ciphers are messages written in rectangular blocks. The message is written one row at a time, and then read off the columns.

TCITNAL HREHGNE EESESE! STOWOA ELNIFG

Frankie tried and tried. It made no sense. She looked at her page of scribbles. Was it her imagination, or was a pattern emerging? She tried one last time.

```
THESE
CRETL
IESON
THEWI
NGSOF
ANEAG
LE!
```

Each column revealed a row of words:

THESECRETLIESONTHEWINGSOFANEAGLE!

Frankie stared again at the page.

THE SECRET LIES ON THE WINGS OF AN EAGLE!

She touched the silver eagles' wings at her throat. When the Commander had mentioned Mission Avalanche, hadn't she said that Chomo Lonzo looked like the wings of an eagle? 'That's where Dad's hidden the trigger key!' Frankie said aloud.

'Turn around and walk backwards very slowly,' said a cold voice behind her. The blood drained from Frankie's face. 'Tell me again where the trigger key is,' a woman said. Ever so slowly, Frankie turned. *Hanna?* If it was her, she looked completely different. Her short grey hair was slicked back. She was dressed in a black ski suit, her gammy leg straight and functional. She also looked about twenty kilos lighter. In her right hand she held a small vial of clear liquid.

Boss went to lunge at Hanna, but Frankie grabbed his collar. 'Not now, boy,' she said. Boss strained, but he obeyed Frankie.

'That spare tyre was really starting to bug me,' Hanna said, patting her flat stomach. 'I've never liked carrying extra weight, especially not an inner tube around my stomach.' Frankie thought of all the times she had hugged Hanna's inner tube, and shuddered.

'What do you want?' Frankie demanded. 'Or should I say, what does the Alliance want?'

Hanna laughed. Frankie used to love Hanna's laugh, but now it sounded menacing. 'Well done, Frankie,' she said. 'I know you've been sneaking around in places you shouldn't be.' Boss wriggled free and bared his teeth at Hanna. 'Get that mutt out of my face. Tell him to back off.'

Frankie hadn't thought this through. She shouldn't have come here alone. Maybe she could keep Hanna talking.

Hanna marched Frankie backwards until her back was against the boathouse doors.

'You and that stupid handbook,' Hanna muttered, plucking it off Frankie's desk. 'I should have thrown it out years ago. I indulged your father far too much. Not to worry,' she added, holding the vial up to the light. 'This truth serum should help immensely.'

So what Tucker had said was true – the Alliance really had made a truth serum.

Frankie walked towards Hanna. She couldn't let the Alliance find out where the trigger key was! 'Take me to my dad!' Frankie demanded.

Hanna laughed and shook her head. 'Your father won't comply with our demands,' Hanna said. 'So instead you will tell me everything.'

'Where is he?'

'In a nice, cosy cell somewhere deep in the Pacific,' Hanna said. 'You'll never see him again,' she said pleasantly, as if she was discussing the weather. 'Now, all we need is the Icefall technology. You wouldn't happen to have it on you?' Hanna snarled, advancing. Frankie could not believe the danger she saw in Hanna's eyes.

'Tell me where Dad is!' Frankie said.

Hanna's eyes turned to steely slits. 'Never!' Hanna said. 'The Alliance is my family. They have always been there for me. I would serve them in any capacity. Even as a housekeeper and,' she sneered '. . . a babysitter.'

'I thought you were my friend,' Frankie said forlornly.

She felt the boathouse door against her back. There was nowhere left for her to go.

'Time to tell me everything, Frankie,' Hanna said, advancing on her with the truth serum. Frankie fumbled in her cargo pocket for the small canister that Miggles had given her that morning. Her fingers clutched at the smooth metal of the tube. Hanna was almost on her. She drew it out, gave Boss a quick nod to get out of the way, found the button, pressed hard and closed her eyes.

For a whole minute, Frankie kept her eyes closed, just as Miggles had instructed. Then she cracked open an eye. Hanna's face had changed into an angry cross-section of lines. Her mouth formed a silent 'O'. She was still as stone, her arm outstretched and frighteningly close to Frankie's face. Then, ever-so-slowly, Hanna toppled over in the very same position. The freeze spray had worked! Miggles was a genius! Frankie opened her eyes. Hanna's eyes were blinking – but her body was completely immobile.

'The victim can see and hear what is happening around them,' Miggles had explained. 'They just can't move for a few hours. Usually giving the agent enough time to restrain them.' Frankie bent to look at Hanna's face. As she leant over, shadows fell across her. Frankie tensed up. *Not more Alliance agents!* But instead, it was Tucker and JJ. They had appeared from nowhere.

'Frankie!' JJ said worriedly. 'Are you alright?'

'Good job, Fox,' Tucker said.

CHAPTER EIGHTEEN

Cryptology is a spy's best friend and an enemy's worst nightmare. Wars can be won or lost using coded messages. The most famous code-making machine was Enigma, invented in Germany at the end of the First World War.

THE SPY'S HANDBOOK

GRIFFIN ESTATE, GRIFFIN CLOSE, HARBOUR CITY
▼

'She was your housekeeper?' JJ asked, looking at Hanna, who was still frozen. 'Wow. She must have been a great operative.'

'To go underground for ten years is remarkable,' Tucker said, his hand on Frankie's shoulder. 'To stay true to her mission would have taken a will of steel.'

'It's actually impressive,' said JJ.

Frankie punched him in the arm.

'Hey!' she said. 'She's one of the bad guys – remember? She said she was going to get the truth out of me no matter what.' Frankie shuddered at the memory.

'The Alliance is famous for its brainwashing ways. They have turned even the toughest agents.' His eyes turned steely. 'Just as well she didn't get to you, Agent Fox. We'll take her back to the Fortress. When the spray wears off, she might be ready to talk.'

It was only then that Frankie remembered the handbook. She was in such a rush that the words tumbled out of her mouth.

'I think I know where the trigger key is. *The Spy's Handbook* is the dead drop – the place where Dad left the top-secret information for me. He's been trying to tell me something all along!'

She picked up the book, and drew Tucker and JJ away from Hanna so the Alliance agent couldn't hear them. 'The secret lies on the wings of an eagle!' Frankie touched the necklace at her throat.

Captain Tucker looked concerned. 'Looks like we're heading to Nepal.'

CHAPTER NINETEEN

Even the best spies can be broken if they feel they have nothing to live for.

THE SPY'S HANDBOOK

ALLIANCE FLOATING BUNKER #1, 60KM WEST OF THE MARIANA TRENCH, NEAR GUAM
▼

For the first time in Fergus Fox's life, he was a man without a plan. He had lived through dozens of missions, and he knew he had so much more to give. Yet here he was, trapped in a steel-lined room with no way out.

All that kept him going was the knowledge that Frankie would find the message, crack the code and get the trigger key. He had sent it to the one person in the world who he could trust to hide it, which was Mr Lo.

He had asked Mr Lo to bury it near the precipice of Chomo Lonzo.

Fear and guilt cut through him like a knife. What if something happened to Frankie? He tried to reassure himself that Griffin would send a rescue mission to save her, at the very least. And Frankie could look after herself. Her years of sleeper training would see to that. His mind spun as he thought about whether he'd made the right decision.

The familiar cold voice spoke to him from across the room.

'It's payback time, honey. Are you ready to tell us where Icefall is?' the woman asked sweetly. 'We promise that no harm will come to Frankie if you do . . .' She laughed, her voice trailing away as she held out a strand of curly blonde hair. Frankie's.

Licking his dry lips, Agent Fergus Fox began to speak. He didn't have any other choice. He would give his interrogator exactly what she wanted.

CHAPTER TWENTY

Spies should be ready to travel at a moment's notice. They always have a bag packed. They can make themselves at home virtually anywhere in the world.

THE SPY'S HANDBOOK

SOMEWHERE OVER THE INDIAN OCEAN
▼

The noise was deafening. Frankie and JJ slapped their headphones on but the racket remained, drowning out any thought. Their khaki flight suits were itchy. Beside them, Captain Tucker looked at home in the giant hold of the plane, packing bags and checking supplies. The three of them were hitching a ride on a Boeing C-17 Globemaster III cargo carrier bound for the Middle East.

Frankie and JJ strapped themselves into the seats at the side of the plane. The crew asked no questions and took no notice of them.

'It's just like *Military Ops* – but real!' exclaimed JJ.

Frankie smiled. He reminded her of Rani. She suddenly realised that she wouldn't be able to tell her best friend about any of this – it would have to stay top-secret. Frankie frowned – she had missed Rani's sleepover. She wondered what Rani, Zan and Cat were doing right now. Probably sitting in a classroom and wondering where she was.

'I still don't know where we'll land,' JJ muttered to Frankie, punching in some numbers on his tablet. 'The airport closest to where we need to be in Nepal is Tenzing-Hillary. Unless there's another airstrip we don't know about; it's too mountainous to land.' He frowned at the topographical map again.

Beside him, Frankie was buried in *The Spy's Handbook.* She made notes on her tablet. Her stomach lurched with the thrum of the engines around her. Boss's whiskers quivered ever-so-slightly.

She prayed, hoped and wished upon a star that JJ's directions to the Alliance bunker were right. Hopefully, her father had already been saved by the rescue unit, a team of paratroopers.

Four hours later, Captain Tucker stood. 'We're nearly there,' he yelled at them through the headphones.

'Lhasa airport?' JJ asked hopefully.

'No go,' Tucker replied. 'Gotta get into the mouth of the Himalayas. It'd take days to get up to Chomo Lonzo from Lhasa. We don't have time. We're going to jump right into Chomo Lonzo.'

'Will Boss be okay?' Frankie asked.

Tucker looked at Boss.

'You kidding? It's not him I'm worried about.' Boss practically smiled. 'He's the smartest dog I've ever met.'

Frankie and JJ listened closely to Tucker's instructions about how to skydive. He showed them how to land in a run and how to land in a roll. He told them – all going well – that the wind would help float them down.

What he did not mention was the fact that they had less than thirty minutes before they jumped out of the cargo hatch into the great white below.

CHAPTER TWENTY-ONE

Spies push themselves to their physical and mental limits. Large people become nimble, light people find strength they never had. Impatient people become patient, and the shiest person in the room can become the most confident.

THE SPY'S HANDBOOK

CLASSIFIED LOCATION, SOMEWHERE ABOVE NEPAL
▼

Frankie had never been very good with heights, but in four minutes time she had to take a running leap out of the back of a cargo plane into the white snow below, down several thousand feet.

'Hatch opening,' said the pilot calmly over the communications system. Frankie was terrified. Spying in her own backyard had been fine, but now she was jumping out of a plane!

Frankie's knuckles were white from gripping her seatbelt. Unsnapping it seemed the least sensible thing to do, but Griffin needed her. Her father had to be saved, and the Icefall technology had to be protected.

JJ fiddled with his parachute pack, then helped Frankie on with hers. Her shoulders sagged. It felt like an elephant had been strapped to her back. Her knees buckled and the thought of flying through the air with it like a lead balloon filled her with dread.

Tucker went through the procedure a final time with them. 'Pull on the right strap, steer with the left,' he said.

Frankie repeated it to herself.

'I'll go first, with Boss strapped to me, and you follow. Stay near me. I'll hit the ground first, then I'll wait for you to arrive.' Tucker shook their hands. For only the second time since they had met him, he smiled. 'Chin up, Agents,' he said. 'You're going to want to do this again and again.'

The hazard lights flashed on and the cargo hatch began to open. Cold air rushed through the hold and the plane slowly shuddered, adjusting to the lower altitude. Tucker turned, gave the thumbs up, placed his goggles over his face and mask and ran at the speed of an Olympic sprinter down the hatch and out.

JJ looked a hundred times worse than carsick. He had a problem telling his left from right sometimes and he hoped that important information didn't fail him right at this moment. 'AGGGGHHHHH!' he screamed as he ran down the gangway and disappeared into thin air.

Frankie wondered if it was too late to chicken out. With wobbly knees and shaking legs, she ran towards the light and jumped. Instead of falling downwards, Frankie felt like she was being pushed upwards. Around

and around she spun in the air. Was she floating, or even moving? The earth seemed far below her.

She remembered one of the things Tucker had told her. She yanked at the right strap of her backpack. For a moment nothing happened. Then her shoulders snapped back and she was falling towards the earth.

Ahead of her she saw two specks drifting in and out of her vision – Tucker and JJ. Colours exploded into life below her. Harsh jagged browns, mixed with soft white. It was the most beautiful thing she'd ever seen in her life, and she was approaching it all at lightning speed.

CHAPTER TWENTY-TWO

A spy can be at their lowest ebb and still find the energy to go on, for the sake of the mission.

THE SPY'S HANDBOOK

CHOMO LONZO MOUNTAIN PASS, NEPAL
▼

The view could have been that of heaven itself. Soft white clouds were pierced by jagged mountaintops – the harsh peaks of Makalu and beyond. Not a finger of civilisation had touched this place. Frankie could only wonder about the hidden Alliance laboratory that had been destroyed eleven years ago by Griffin on her parents' final mission together.

Where the mountains lined up, a silhouette looked familiar. Together, the three peaks across the valley formed what looked like the wings of an eagle. JJ, Tucker and Frankie followed the trail upward. Frankie pulled her spectacles from her pocket.

'I hope Miggles was right,' she murmured. She slipped them on and zoomed in. Brown and white fuzz appeared but then the lens sharpened and she made out two small hills.

'At last,' Agent Frankie Fox said. 'The secret really does lie on the wings of an eagle.'

•

As they made their way up to the two hills, Frankie and JJ's breath slowed. The altitude made breathing difficult, and so they had to walk slowly, even though all they wanted to do was find the trigger key and get out of the cold.

Captain Tucker led the way, his eyes peeled for any sign of the Alliance. It seemed as though they were alone. The only footprints they saw were their own. Still, they remained wary. You could never trust the Alliance.

Frankie was exhausted. It had been not even two full days since she and JJ had kayaked out to the Fortress. School was a forgotten memory. She felt like a survivor, on her own, without her father and Hanna. She would deal with the knowledge of Hanna's treachery later, when she had time. For now, she focused on the steep mountain terrain around them, following in JJ's footsteps and using him as a windbreak.

'Stay focused,' Captain Tucker warned. Here and there, ice patches had formed, and it was very cold. Boss scampered ahead. 'We'll go straight through.' The mountainside narrowed and was growing increasingly hard to climb. JJ's legs were stiffening up. It was wonderful just stopping for even a few seconds.

'C'mon!' Frankie urged. 'We need to hurry!'

•

The Alliance had released Agent Fergus Fox, but instead of returning him to Harbour City, he now found himself once again in the Kangshung valley. He lay heavily on the grass, his fingers feeling their way over his broken ribs. In the back of his mind, he wondered if Griffin had sent a rescue unit to the bunker. But it was too late now, they'd never find him here.

He had been thrown out of the chopper and his mouth felt full of mountain dust and dirt. He cracked an eye open and the world spun into focus. The three peaks of Chomo Lonzo lined up, and a flash of hope shot through him. Only one thought willed him on.

Frankie could be nearby. He might be imagining things, but had he heard a dog barking that sounded just like Boss?

Where was his precious daughter? Gingerly, he pushed himself to a sitting position. Every bone in his body felt broken. He staggered to his feet, his nerves tingling. He had to find the Alliance agent and take her down. And he had to see Frankie.

Agent Fergus Fox gritted his teeth, flexed his muscles and started the slow, painful journey up the mountainside.

CHAPTER TWENTY-THREE

An agent that has been 'turned' can go rogue. It should be noted that their true allegiance is usually to themselves.

THE SPY'S HANDBOOK

CHOMO LONZO MOUNTAIN PASS, NEPAL

▼

Boss growled. Frankie stared. It couldn't be. A living piece of evidence stood in front of her, breathing heavily.

They were at the final resting place of the trigger key. And the Alliance had beaten them there.

'Don't move,' the woman said, walking down the icy mountain path towards Frankie. She held a small pouch at her side. It must have held the trigger key. The woman glanced at Tucker and JJ. 'The girl comes with me. Alone,' she said.

Tucker grimaced and JJ grabbed at Frankie's arm.

Boss barked loudly, and dashed to Frankie's side. 'It's okay,' Frankie said, shrugging out of JJ's grip.

Tucker tensed, ready for a fight.

Frankie took a deep breath and stepped towards the woman.

Light bounced off the snow of the valley, momentarily blinding Frankie. The woman was walking further up the hill, towards the edge. Frankie followed her, picking the same footsteps as the woman but following at a safe pace.

Then the woman turned. Her eyes were so familiar it was like looking in the mirror. Instinctively, Frankie moved towards her.

'Don't come any closer,' the woman growled. Her white-blonde hair tumbled across her face and down her back, a holster strapped around her black turtleneck sweater. The pouch holding the trigger key bag dangled at her side. Frankie's mind played out a range of options. How could she get her hands on that pouch?

'Payback is a beautiful thing,' the woman said.

'Joanna?' Frankie croaked.

'Don't you know how to properly address your mother? How about *Mum*?' Her voice was crisp and

clear. But not a single sliver of motherly warmth oozed out of the woman. From this angle, Frankie could see that she was still beautiful, her sharp nose and green, almond-shaped eyes standing out against her olive skin. Eyes that matched Frankie's.

'Mum?' Frankie echoed shakily. The word sounded so unfamiliar. She realised that she had never said the word out loud before.

The woman laughed harshly.

'Too late, Francesca,' she said sweetly.

'My name's Frankie,' said Frankie defiantly. The woman stiffened. Frankie saw Joanna Fox's defences fail her for a moment. 'You make me sick!' she felt the words come burbling out of her. 'How can you work for the Alliance? They kidnapped Dad!'

Joanna Fox reeled like she had been slapped across the face.

'Don't you care about your family?' Frankie cried, advancing up the path. She was so close to touching her mother.

'You're not my family!' Joanna Fox responded. 'I was supposed to be a mother. Griffin left me behind!' By now Frankie was close enough to see into her mother's eyes. Something strange was going on. Joanna's eyes were blank and unseeing. *Almost like she had been brainwashed . . .*

'You left me behind,' Joanna said, her voice cold.

'I was a baby, Mum,' Frankie cried. If she could only touch her, if she could only make her mother see that she still loved her, that she had never stopped loving her or wanting her to be alive . . .

The word 'Mum' jolted Joanna Fox back to reality. Frankie reached out but her mother stiffened and pulled away, out of reach. Her arms hung limply by her side. Staring at Frankie, Joanna Fox fell to her knees and dropped the pouch. She opened her mouth, but no words came out. When she did speak, it was as though she was talking to herself. 'I thought I could turn Fergus. Get him to join the Alliance. But your father is strong . . . and he needs you. He told me himself, in the bunker.'

The woman looked into her daughter's eyes. Slowly, Joanna rose once again to her feet. This is it, Frankie thought. My first hug . . .

'Mum?' she said again.

Joanna Fox reacted instantly – almost as though the Alliance had flicked a switch inside her. Blinking rapidly, she turned and ran as fast as she could to the rocky ledge teetering over Chomo Lonzo. Without a backwards glance, she took a flying leap and sailed over, plummeting through the sky. Frankie tried to run up the mountain, a scream dying in her throat and her legs feeling like lead. She bent over, taking deep gulps of air, trying to stop the tremors running through her body. She heard voices behind her, but still Frankie inched closer and closer to the edge.

Boss, Tucker and JJ rushed up the precipice, hoping that Frankie was safe. Not far away, Fergus Fox ran towards the commotion. He had Tucker and JJ in his sights now. He'd been right about Boss! They all pushed up the hill.

Fergus Fox flew past Tucker, JJ and Boss, adrenalin kicking in. He saw Frankie lying on the ground up above him, and his heart jumped into his mouth. He threw himself to the ground. *Please, let her be alive*, he thought.

An arm came down on Frankie's shoulder, shaking her hard. She looked up into her father's eyes.

'DAD!' Frankie cried, clutching him. She staggered to her feet and hugged him as tight as she could. She never wanted to let go. Tears ran down her cheeks.

'Thank god you're safe . . . Agent Fox,' he said. 'You got my message, didn't you?'

Frankie beamed. 'Yes, Dad. I cracked the code!' Then she paled.

'Mum . . .' Frankie managed to say, pointing to the deep valley below. Fergus nodded. Joanna – his lucky Jo – had forced him to hand over the location of the trigger key and then abandoned him.

JJ and Tucker moved to the edge. Boss wound himself around Frankie's legs, licking her ankles. 'Look!' JJ cried. Frankie and Fergus turned to look at the vast Kangshung valley below them. A large black parachute sailed across the thermals, gliding across the valley. Joanna Fox had BASE jumped into the mouth of the Chomo Lonzo pass – back into the arms of her beloved Alliance. They all watched as the black sail grew smaller and smaller against the blinding glare of the white snow. A faint hope beat within Frankie's heart.

She held out the pouch to her father and to Captain Tucker. 'Mum left this behind. It's the trigger key,' Frankie said, her voice cracking.

She looked at her dad with fresh eyes. Gone was the businessman in the sharp suit. Even in his dishevelled state, Frankie saw that he had the heart of a Griffin warrior. She burst with pride. Whatever lay ahead for them both, she knew that they would get through it. Together. Her mother had told her that. Her father needed her. And she needed him.

'Mission Icefall is complete,' Captain Tucker broke in. Then he turned to look at her father. 'You alright, Fergus?' he said.

Agent Fergus Fox nodded. 'Let's call this in.'

JJ and Frankie stood together at the edge of the cliff. Boss, too, stood proud.

'We did it,' JJ whispered, smiling at Frankie.

A rush of pride and excitement surged through Frankie. Together with her new friend and fellow agent JJ, she had changed the course of history. Life would never be the same again now she was a real spy. She thought of Rani. Was she going to be able to tell her best friend about all this?

'It's not over yet, JJ,' Frankie trailed off, her heart-beat finally returning to normal. Her eyes hunted for the last sign of her mother, but the black speck was gone.

Joanna Fox was long gone. There and then, on the roof of the world, Agent Frankie Fox made a secret promise to herself that she would do everything possible to find her mother again. In fact, she would make it her mission.

Yvette Poshoglian is the author of more than a dozen books for kids. A high school English teacher, she also runs creative writing workshops, consults to publishers and educational organisations on literacy, communications and information technology, and speaks at writers' festivals, library events and schools. Yvette is based in Sydney, Australia.

yvetteposhoglian.com
facebook.com/yvetteposhoglianauthor
twitter.com/yvetteposh

**Look out for Frankie's
next amazing adventure,
Operation Boy Band –
coming soon!**

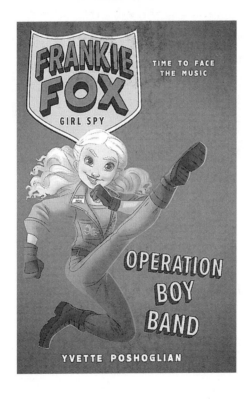

CHILDREN'S BOOKS

If you would like to find out more about
Hachette Children's Books, our authors, upcoming
events and new releases you can visit our website,
Facebook or follow us on Twitter:

www.hachettechildrens.com.au
www.twitter.com/HCBoz
www.facebook.com/hcboz